Khyrus

DEITY

of Virtue &

Strength

To avenge his fallen parents and to preserve what they've fought to protect, Khyrus must defeat Nirjin, God of Destruction. His people are depending on his uprising. His people are strong and determined to withstand the hardships being brought onto them until their rightful leader returns. Khyrus' heart is good but, will he have the strength? The will?

Published by Rachel Griffin, Founder of Pen & Camera.

To Zion, who has inspired me to share my thoughts with the world. I love you and like you. I appreciate you? Continue to do and be great.

To my inner circle, I like to call my family. For all your continuous support and love I am grateful. I love and appreciate you all.

Contents

Who is Khyrus?

Khyrus was born on Planet Ebon. His parents are the Leaders of the Ebone'a Realm. He was named after his mother and father. Khyra is the Deity of Virtue and Thorus is the Deity of Strength. They want Khyrus to be both virtuous and strong. Not just physically, but mentally as well. Only knowing how to fight wouldn't be enough. Knowing when and why to fight had to be instilled in him. His parents knew he would utilize both, but have a life partner to assist.

Khyrus and his people train their minds and bodies every morning. If they were not acquiring the knowledge of self-defense, they were guided on how to survive WITH each other. They were always kept busy being filled with knowledge. Khyrus knew he would be the next leader after his parents. He would attempt to train harder than others. There was no doubt he would be great like his parents. His parents, ancestors, and the efforts of those who supported his family would be in vain if he didn't.

The Planet Ebon is beautiful. Everything flows in balance with nature. The homes and businesses are built in the source. Ebon's natural beasts and the Ebonee's people all live together in unity. Conflict was a rarity. Most were handled through finding a middle ground. One day their peace was disrupted by a people so ruthless mercy is a cursed word in their language.

Pale Skinned beasts named "Neanderans" from the planet Ander'a invaded Ebon to claim it as their own. Instead of talking things out with Khyra and Thorus, Nirjin, Deity of Destruction, wanted to take everything by force. "You have a planet in your own realm. Why do you want to claim ours?" asked Khyra as she and Thorus stood in front of their castle. The children ran inside while the civilians scattered. Nirjin laughed and said:

> My entire realm, let alone my planet, isn't anywhere NEAR good enough for us. We want more. But, I would rather have someone else do all the work while we relax. Your people work hard to preserve your home and protect each other. By us taking over, it'll be a win-win situation. We get your home and you'll be my Brown Imps. It'll be perfect!

Nirjin, Khyra, and Thorus engaged in battle. Many elders were captured. The children escaped into the tunnel below the castle. Khyrus stayed behind underneath the hidden door to watch their fight. He didn't want his home to be in Nirjins' control. He wanted everyone to be happy. Live the way they always have. Not having a leader who's for himself. Khyrus watches with heart and tears full of anger as Nirjin defeats his parents. The worst has happened. He makes his way to their underground temple with heartbreaking news.

Stronger Than Ancestors

Khyrus finally arrives at the temple. Leona, his best friend, asks what happened. Wiping away tears, Khyrus responds "My parents are gone. Nirjin has begun taking over. The elders are now his Brown Imps. We're the only ones left who could fight." The children began to cry. Leona, now angry, yells "we don't stand a chance against him! We aren't strong enough yet!" Khyrus sighs and says "I know. That's why we'll have to train and conjure up a plan to get them out." He guaranteed there would be unity and peace returned to Ebon. That they'd become stronger than those before them. They'd make them proud.

Khyrus wished to be a magnificent leader. Now more than ever. Aside from The Most High, Creator of Life, he loves his people and home more than anything. All who share his home know he stands for the good and balance of their home.

The children were reassured that over the next twelve years, they will have the power to reclaim what was rightfully theirs. Each day, they would train while coming up with strategies to end Nirjins' reign. The last thing they wished for is for their future generations to suffer as they have. Once they agreed on a plan, they discussed each person's role and tasks. Leona is a negotiator who began taking up archery. After some training, she announced "I'm becoming more comfortable with being molded into a warrior. I wish to use these skills to fend off the Neanders." All the children celebrated her words of comfort.

Khyrus admired her bravery. He ended the meeting with: "We'll become stronger than our past selves and wiser than our ancestors. Learning from our errors is just as important as learning from others' mistakes." There was nothing Khyrus wouldn't do to regain what was stolen. Mother Ebon and her children shouldn't be treated this way. During all of this, there was someone he looked to for inspiration.

Be My Wife and Lead with Me

At age sixteen, Khyrus was becoming more intrigued by Leona. In two years, she would have been appointed by the elders as Deity of Intelligence. Khyrus wished for her to be by his side in the kingdom. His emotions are a hindrance when making decisions while Leona was content. She is versatile in communicating with all beings of life.

Khyrus acquired the strength and knowledge to keep the balance on his home world with all that survive and live on Ebon. Although Khyrus has a strong will, he lacks critical thought. Without Leona, he wouldn't have become such a great leader. She gave him the knowledge of patience and clear communication. Their bond over time has grown exponentially. Before they rested, words were shared.

Leona shares what is on her mind with her people. "With unity, honor, trust, and loyalty, we will become

unstoppable. Brothers and sisters of Ebon, our bond WILL thrive as we grow into a stronger unit and family."
She cries when the Ebone'a people feel helpless. With all that is going on, Leona still stands strong and brave. Khyrus responds with:

> "I wish for this to happen more than you can imagine. The years we have spent here will not be in vain. Soon we will claim what is rightfully ours. My love, soon we shall bond our souls and you will become my Empress."

"Rise of the Ebon Sun" was going to be the name of the day they are reclaiming their home. They announce their union as well as settle on plans for travel to the above world. They trust in equal exchange as much as their success. Get back what you put in while giving out of kindness. Meanwhile, Nirjin was enjoying reaping the benefits of others.

Nirjins' Rule

Within twelve years, the Neanderans have turned Ebon upside down. The planet, once beautiful and peaceful, is now filled with destruction. Nirjin made Thorus crown his own but kept the other one and both thrones. The temple and castle are in shambles. The natives of the land are broken down spiritually. They went from living humble lifestyles to living as though they were less than beasts. All living beings were able to coexist. There would be little to no conflict.

Ebonea's would only receive gifts from Mother Ebon only in prayer of love and appreciation for the life given to them. All gifts were used to the fullest extent of their existence. In return, they would protect Ebon from all those who seek her destruction. Trade was the only necessity, for money had no value. Greed was never in their hearts. Neanderans are the opposite. Greed is a code of law in their minds. They would trade with items of lesser value than what is offered to them.

Like most from the Pale'a Realm, Nirjin is a corrupted leader. He rules with fear, violence, and false ideologies. He's killed the Eboneas that have attempted to rebel against him. Nirjin screams "this is my land now! Follow and live or defy and die! There's no in-between!"

His speech bellowed as if he were speaking to the entire realm. His words and actions caused Mother Ebon to become unbalanced. She became furious and summoned monstrous storms to destroy all those who sought her destruction. She knew her children would return. She continued her retaliation in aid of the Eboneas to guarantee their victory.

Like most battles Neanderans have faced, the root of this was Greed and Envy. The thought of not having what the Eboneas had angered Nirjin, so he used those sins to justify his evil deeds.

Greed & Envy

The Neanderans are wasteful and destructive. They feel the need to take from others. Especially if they're happy and prosperous, unlike them. Nirjin uses those sins to gain what he wants. Sadly, his people follow without question.

Nirjin had taken notice of how Khyrus' people had been living and how much joy they had in their hearts. He made it clear what his goals were when he said to his followers "we shall crush their will and destroy their happiness. For we shall be the only ones who bask in the glory of joyfulness."

On their home planet Palea, Nirjin concocted a plan to conquer the Eboneas homeland. He concluded that Khyra and Thorus must be destroyed for his plan to be the ruler of Ebon. The people in this realm were his prey. He was the predator. Khyra and Thorus fought well against Nirjin but failed. Thorus looked into Nirjins eyes and his final words were:

> "Though you've succeeded now, you won't win in the end. Our children will rise. Our people will be free and Mother Ebon will be healthy again. Your people have failed since the dawn of your sorry existence and you'll fail again."

Nirjin beheads them. He holds both of their heads in front of his followers as a trophy. He shouts "On the day of the return of the children of THESE worthless creatures, we shall also put their heads on a stake. They were wise enough to run when they had the chance." He put their heads on posts and burned their bodies. All the children escaped through a route that leads to Khyrus' family temple. Nirjin stood outside the castle looking across the horizon with pride knowing what he had accomplished for himself. This sunfall symbolizes the end of what was and the beginning of misery.

Rising of the Ebon Sun

On Khyrus' eighteenth birthday, he and his companions made their way to the castle. Nirjin was outside glaring at his new Brown Imps. As he sat on his throne, Leona shot an arrow into his shoulder from behind. Nirjin angrily turned and yelled for his guards. "They're dead. Don't bother" Leona said to him. Nirjin threatens their lives as he yells for the Neanderans. Leona led her comrades to fight against them.

Nirjin exclaims that they won't succeed. He attempts to attack them at the door. Khyrus stands in his path. "Where did you come from?!" Nirjin yells in anger and confusion. Khyrus answers "Like my parents told you years ago, we're going to rise and claim what's ours! You don't deserve any of this. This is our Rising of the Ebon Sun! My people shall be released from captivity and enslavement!"

Nirjin lets out an ear-aching scream. It was almost deafening. His blood is boiling as he turns rose red. Khyrus balls up his fists prepared to fight. Nirjin grabs his knife and rock and charges Khyrus. Who will prevail? Khyrus, fighting for peace, justice, and harmony? Or Nirjin, fighting for lies, fear, and greed? Planet Ebons' survival depends on Khyrus.

Fight for What's Just!

Leona and her friends defeated the Neanderans. Most of them retreated to the Pale'a Realm. Their demise was inevitable. They soon preferred to die the slow, miserable death they also deserved. The Eboneas succeeded in taking back their home and became superior in the battle. But, know that the war may not be over. The remaining Neanderans boarded their ship and left as fast as they could.

Leona and her comrades treated their elders' injuries. A woman said to her "I never saw you as a fighter. You were always such a chatterbox. An extremely knowledgeable chatterbox.". At that same moment, Nirjin took the position Khyrus' parents had years ago. Khyrus towered over him. Nirjin asks "Why continue to fight? You've won." He had the look of defeat and fear, something he never showed before. Khyrus grabs Nirjins' weapon as he and Leona said:

"I fought to protect and defend from all foes. We fight for what is ours and just. That can be done verbally and physically. This was a rare moment where fists had to be used. I was protecting what I love: my home and people, peace, and everything we trust in. That's something I'll always do. As long as I survive, I'll make sure to keep to my word."

Leona tightens the elders' bandage as Khyrus beheads Nirjin. Khyrus walks out with Nirjins' head. Leona joins him and holds it high by his thinning hair. Khyrus informs his people "this moment symbolizes what will never happen again. We, as your new leader, Emperor, and Empress, will make sure of it". From that day forward, his word was kept. The changes their people wished and prayed for were beginning to happen.

New Beginning

After many repairs, Mother Ebon begins to revive all of the life that has been destroyed by Nirjin and his army. All life on Ebon began to thrive again in peace and harmony. The elders were proud of their people for what they have accomplished. The children of their fellow elders have grown to be brave and powerful. Freedom was what they wished for. With the help of all the Eboneas youth and leadership, they were able to see their wish manifested.

Leona and Khyrus birthed their first child which was a beautiful Ebone'a little girl they named Thyra. As she grows, she will have gained the knowledge of knowing she was born in a family of brave, strong, morally sound deities. Future generations have learned the ways of their people. They gained the inspiration to do better than those before them. Acquiring knowledge from the mistakes of the past. While the children learned through exposure, Khyrus and Leona were able to implement strategies to keep the negative energies at bay. The three of them stood in the center of Broken Shields, their meeting grounds. Khyrus says:

> "I take joy in making our ancestors proud and keeping a promise I've made. Mostly because I proved my parents correct. The bonds we were able to create with each other are magnificent. I pray that those who have transcended before us look down and smile. No evil shall prosper."

Strength in virtue will always be greater than Greed and Envy.

Authors Note

This story came about after some conversations with my husband, Zion. We talked about the numerous Gads and Deities that exist. Mentioned how they all still live in various places and forms and most of us being the essence of Gads/Deities. Others live elsewhere because of their frustration with the majority of the beings that inhabit it (mankind and some humans).

That conversation is what inspired me to come up with the idea to not only write a fantasy novel about them but to create my own as well. I also wanted to get across valuable lessons by the time readers reach the end of the novel. I began by coming up with various names and combining some of those names. Making them Gads and Gaddesses of various things was a lot simpler because I based them on various personality traits.

Combining the names of certain characters allowed me to be able to start small families. The combined names would be the children. The names that weren't combined were the parents/elders. After many months spent reigniting my inspiration and motivation, decision-making, and pages upon pages of notes, I began to write what became my first full novel. This is an accomplishment I thought I wouldn't achieve, but I'm proud of myself for pushing myself to do this. I have outside sources to thank as well and I'm grateful for them being there.

I wrote this story to show people what happens when we unite. We're stronger together. Because of that, mankind is afraid and rather has us divided. Not acquire the knowledge and the drive needed to make great things happen. If we want change, WE have to be responsible for whether that change occurs. Be a combination of MLK and Malcolm X: know when to raise your voice and fist.